OUR LITTLE HUNGARIAN COUSIN

MARY F. NIXON ROULET

Our Little Hungarian Cousin

CHAPTER I

WITH THE TZIGANES

BANDA BELA, the little Gypsy boy, had tramped all day through the hills, until, footsore, weary, and discouraged, he was ready to throw himself down to sleep. He was very hungry, too.

"I shall go to the next hilltop and perhaps there is a road, and some passerby will throw me a crust. If not, I can feed upon my music and sleep," he thought to himself, as he clambered through the bushes to the top of the hill. There he stood, his old violin held tight in his scrawny hand, his ragged little figure silhouetted against the sky.

Through the central part of Hungary flows in rippling beauty the great river of the Danube. Near to Kecskés the river makes a sudden bend, the hills grow sharper in outline, while to the south and west sweep the great grass plains.

Before Banda Bela, like a soft green sea, the Magyar plain stretched away until it joined the horizon in a dim line. Its green seas of grain were cut only by the tall poplar trees which stood like sentinels against the sky. Beside these was pitched a Gypsy camp, its few tents and huts huddled together, looking dreary and forlorn in the dim twilight. The little hovels were built of bricks and stones and a bit of thatch, carelessly built to remain only until the wander spirit rose again in their breasts and the Gypsies went forth to roam the green velvet plain, or float down the Danube in their battered old boats, lazily happy in the sun.

In front of the largest hut was the fire-pot, slung from a pole over a fire of sticks burning brightly. The Gypsies were gathered about the fire for their evening meal, and the scent of goulash came from the kettle. Banda Bela could hardly stand from faintness, but he raised his violin to his wizened chin and struck a long chord. As the fine tone of the old violin smote the night air, the Gypsies ceased talking and looked up. Unconscious of their scrutiny, the boy played a czardas, weird and strange. At first there was a cool, sad strain like the night song of some bird, full of the gentle sadness of those without a home, without friends, yet not without kindness; then the time changed, grew quicker and quicker until it seemed as if the old violin danced itself, so full of wild Gypsy melody were its strains. Fuller and fuller they rose; the bow in the boy's fingers seeming to skim like a bird over the strings. The music, full of wild longing, swelled until its voice rose like the wild scream of some forest creature, then crashed to a full stop. The violin dropped to the boy's side, his eyes closed, and he fell heavily to the ground.

When Banda Bela opened his eyes he found himself lying upon the ground beside the Gypsy fire, his head upon a bundle of rags. The first thing his eyes fell upon was a little girl about six years old, who was trying to put into his mouth a bit of bread soaked in gravy. The child was dressed only in a calico frock, her head was uncovered, her hair, not straight and black like that of the other children who swarmed about, but light as corn silk, hung loosely about her face. Her skin was as dark as sun and wind make the Tziganes, but the eyes which looked into his with a gentle pity were large and deep and blue.

"Who are you?" he asked, half conscious.

"Marushka," she answered simply. "What is your name?"

"Banda Bela," he said faintly.

"Why do you play like the summer rain on the tent?" she demanded.

"Because the rain is from heaven on all the Tziganes, and it is good, whether one lies snug within the tent or lifts the face to the drops upon the heath."

"I like you, Banda Bela," said little Marushka. "Stay with us!"

"That is as your mother wills," said Banda Bela, sitting up.

"I have no mother, though her picture I wear always upon my breast," she said. "But I will ask old Jarnik, for all he says the others do," and she sped away to an old Gypsy, whose gray hair hung in matted locks upon his shoulders. In a moment she was back again, skimming like a bird across the grass.

"SEARCHED THROUGH BANDA BELA WITH A KEEN GLANCE."

"Jarnik says you are to eat, for hunger tells no true tale," she said.

"I am glad to eat, but I speak truth," said Banda Bela calmly.

He ate from the fire-pot hungrily, dipping the crust she gave him into the stew and scooping up bits of meat and beans.

"I am filled," he said at length. "I will speak with Jarnik."

Marushka danced across the grass in front of him like a little will-o'-the-wisp, her fair locks floating in the breeze, in the half light her eyes shining like the stars which already twinkled in the Hungarian sky.

The Gypsy dogs bayed at the moon,

hanging like a crescent over the crest of the hill and silvering all with its calm radiance. Millions of fireflies flitted over the plain, and the scent of the ripened grain was fresh upon the wind.

Banda Bela sniffed the rich, earthy smell, the kiss of the wind was kind upon his brow; he was fed and warm.

"Life is sweet," he murmured. "In the Gypsy camp is brother kindness. If they will have me, I will stay."

Old Jarnik had eyes like needles. They searched through Banda Bela with a keen glance and seemed to pierce his heart.

"The Gypsy camp has welcome for the stranger," he said at length. "Will you stay?"

"You ask me nothing," said Banda Bela, half surprised, half fearing, yet raising brave eyes to the stern old face.

"I have nothing to ask," said old Jarnik. "All I wish to know you have told me."

"But I have said nothing," said Banda Bela.

"Your face to me lies open as the summer sky. Its lines I scan. They tell me of hunger, of weariness and loneliness, things of the wild. Nothing is there of the city's evil. You may stay with us and know hunger no longer. This one has asked for you," and the old man laid his hand tenderly upon little Marushka's head. "You are hers, your only care to see that no harm comes to these lint locks. The child is dear to me. Will you stay?"

"I will stay," said Banda Bela, "and I will care for the child as for my sister. But first I will speak, since I have nothing to keep locked."

"Speak, then," said the old man. Though his face was stern, almost fierce, there was a gentle dignity about him and the boy's heart warmed to him.

"Of myself I will tell you all I know," he said. "I am Banda Bela, son of Šafařik, dead with my mother. When the camp fell with the great red sickness I alone escaped. Then was I ten years old. Now I am fourteen. Since then I have wandered, playing for a crust, eating seldom, sleeping beneath the stars, my clothes the gift of passing kindness. Only my violin I kept safe, for my father had said it held always life within its strings. 'Not only food, boy,' he said, 'but joy and comfort and thoughts of things which count for more than bread.' So I lived with it, my only friend. Now I have two more, you—" he flashed a swift glance at the old man, "and this little one. I will serve you well."

"You are welcome," said old Jarnik, simply. "Now, go to sleep."

Little Marushka, who had been listening to all that had been said, slipped her hand in his and led him away to the boys' tent. She did not walk, but holding one foot in her hand, she hopped along like a gay little bird, chattering merrily.

"I like you, Banda Bela, you shall stay."

CHAPTER II

ALONG THE GYPSY TRAIL

BANDA BELA found life in the Gypsy camp quiet, but not unpleasant. He had a place to sleep and food to eat. Jarnik was good to him and Marushka his devoted friend. Rosa, a young and very pretty Gypsy girl, was kind to the waif, and the rest of the tribe paid no attention to him. What was one ragged boy, more or less, to them? The camp fairly swarmed with them.

Since the Tziganes had crossed the mountains from India many hundred years ago, they had wandered about Hungary, and the Gypsies to whom Banda Bela had come were of the Gletecore, or wandering Gypsies, a better race than the Kortoran who dwell in mud huts or caves near the villages.

The Gletecore are never still. They wander from one end of Hungary to the other, playing their music, begging, stealing, sometimes carving little utensils out of wood, or tinkering for the living which seems to come to them easily, perhaps because they want but little.

There was little that Banda Bela could do, but he waited upon old Jarnik, ran errands, watched Marushka, and caught many a fine fish from the river for the fire-pot. The Danube was full of fish, delicious in flavour.

Always the little boy could make music, and his violin charmed many an hour for him, while Marushka, ever following at his heels like a little dog, learned to love his music scarcely less than he did.

One morning Marushka wakened Banda Bela by calling loudly:

"Banda Bela! Come! The sun is up. Stepan has come back, and they move the camp to-day!"

Banda Bela sprang to his feet and hurried out of the tent. Already there were signs of stir in the camp. Stepan, a young Gypsy chief, was standing beside the cart which was being loaded with camp utensils. Banda Bela had not seen him before, for the chief had been away from the band ever since the boy came.

Stepan was six feet tall; part of his coal-black hair was braided into a tight knob over his forehead, the rest hung down in matted, oily locks upon his shoulders. In his mouth was a long Weixel-wood pipe, and he wore a loose, white, cotton shirt gathered around the neck, and baggy white trousers. He was very handsome and his copper-coloured skin shone as if it was polished. All about him swarmed children and dogs, while the older Gypsies were packing up the camp effects and loading them into the two or three carts, which patient horses stood ready to draw.

"Eat quickly," cried Marushka. "There is but a crust left, I saved it for you. We go on the road to-day, and hunger will gnaw your stomach before we camp again." Banda Bela took the food, ate it hurriedly, and ran up to Stepan.

"Let me help," he said briefly.

"Who are you and what can you do?" the young chief looked him over keenly.

"I am Banda Bela. I can make music with my violin, swing an adze, cut bowls from wood, drive a horse, row a boat, catch fish, do as I am bid, and keep my tongue silent," he said.

"If you can do the last two things you have already learned much," said Stepan. "Go and help Jarnik load, for he is old and feels himself young."

Banda Bela nodded and went over to where the old man was loading one of the carts. He helped as best he could and soon the wagons were loaded and the camp deserted. The Gypsies had taken the road. It was a beautiful day. The wind blew cool and free from the river, which swept along at the foot of wooded heights, gleaming like glass in the morning sun. Ducks splashed in the water, and now and then Banda Bela saw the waters boil and bubble. Something black would flash above the surface, there would be a splash and a swirl of waters, and the radiating ripples reached the shore as a great fish would spring into the air, flash in the sunlight, and sink into the waters again.

Steamers passed down the stream on their way to Buda-Pest, or towing huge barges filled with the peasants' teams and wagons, loaded with grain to be ground at the quaint water mills, built on piles out in the stream where the current was so strong as to turn the huge wheels quickly and grind the grain, raised on the great plains of the south. To the north the mountains rose blue and beautiful. The boy saw all. His eyes shone; his cheek was flushed.

"Good is the Gypsy trail," he said to himself. "Sun, light, and wind, all free, and I am with mine own people. Life is sweet."

All day long the carts rumbled along. When the sun was high overhead the Gypsies rested beside the river. Banda Bela caught some fish, and Rosa cooked them for supper.

Next day they turned from the river and travelled over the plains. There was no shade. To the right stretched great fields of maize and flax. The dust was white and fine, and so hot it seemed almost to prick their faces like needles. It rose in white clouds around the carts and followed them in whirling columns.

In front of them from time to time other clouds of dust arose, which, upon nearing, they discovered to be peasant carts, driven with four or six horses, for the peasants in this part of Hungary are rich and prosperous. The soil is fertile and yields wonderful crops, though for ninety years it has had no rest, but the peasants are not tempted to laziness by the ease with which things grow. They begin their day's work at three o'clock in the morning and work until eight or nine at night, eating their luncheon and supper in the fields.

Banda Bela saw many of them, fine, tall fellows, working easily and well, but in his heart he was glad that he did not have to toil under the hot sun.

Shepherds were seated here and there in the fields, looking like small huts, for they wore queer conical bundas which covered them from their necks to their knees. These sheepskin coats are worn both winter and summer, for the shepherds say they keep out heat as well as cold.

The shepherds must watch the flocks by day and night, and when the weather is wet they sleep sitting on small round stools to keep them from the damp ground. Toward dark the Gypsy band halted by the roadside, near to a group of shepherds' huts. Here they were to stop for the night and Banda Bela was glad, for his legs ached with fatigue. He had walked nearly all day except for a short time when Marushka had asked to have him ride in the cart and play for her.

The shepherds greeted the Tziganes kindly. Jews and Armenians the Hungarians dislike, but for the Gypsies there is a fellow feeling, for all Hungarians love music and nearly all Tziganes have music at their fingers' ends and in their velvet voices.

The Gypsies pitched their tents and Banda Bela stole aside from the camp to play his beloved violin. He tuned it and then gently ran his bow up and down the strings and began a soft little melody. It was like the crooning song of a young mother to her child. The boy was a genius, playing with wonderful correctness and with a love for music which showed in every note he sounded. The shepherds paused in preparing their evening meal and listened. When he ceased playing they called to him, "If you will play more you may eat with us."

"I will play gladly, and gladly will I eat," he answered, showing in a gleaming smile his teeth, even and white as a puppy's. In the pockets of the shepherds' coats were stored all manner of good things, bacon, black bread, and wine, even slivowitz, the wonderfully good Hungarian brandy, which Banda Bela had tasted only once in his life, but which the Gypsies make to perfection.

The shepherds' camp had a one-roomed, straw-thatched hut, which they used as a storehouse for their coats and extra food supplies. A great well was in front of the hut. It had a huge beam of wood with a cross-piece at the top and from this hung a bucket. The boy drew up a bucketful of the water and found it deliciously cold.

Near the camp was the shepherds' cooking hut, made of reeds tied together and with a hole in the top for the escape of the smoke. The hut looked like a corn shock with a door in one side. This door was open and Banda Bela saw a fire burning brightly, a pot hung over the embers, and a smell ofkasa arose, as a tall shepherd tossed the meal and bacon into a kind of cake.

Marushka had strayed away from the Gypsies and now stood beside Banda Bela shyly watching the cooking in silence. She was a quiet little thing, with her golden hair unlike the bold, black-eyed little Gypsy children who rolled around the ground, half clad, snatching food from the pot and gnawing bones like hungry dogs.

"Who is this child?" asked one of the shepherds. "She is no Gypsy. What is your name, child?"

"I am Marushka," she answered sweetly. "Who are you?"

"I am a shepherd," he said, smiling at her.

"Do you tend sheep all day?" she demanded.

"No, once I was one of the juhasz, but now I am past that. I am one of the gulyas, and in another year I shall be among the csikos."

"Where are your oxen?" asked Marushka.

"There in the plain," he said, pointing to what looked like a great, still, white sea some distance away. As he spoke the sea seemed to break into waves, first rippling, then stormy, as the oxen rose to their feet, many of them tossing their heads in the air and bellowing loudly. They were immense creatures, perfectly white and very beautiful, with great dark eyes and intelligent faces.

"There are my children," said the shepherd. "But I am afraid there is a wind storm coming, for they show fear only of storm or fire." He watched the herd for a few moments, but though they snuffed the air they finally settled down quietly to rest again.

"Let us eat," said the shepherd. "Perhaps the storm has passed over."

How good the kasa tasted. The little Tziganes had never eaten it before, and they enjoyed it thoroughly.

The sun was sinking in the west, and the yellow fields of grain were gleaming as if tipped with gold. Dusk deepened, stars peeped out of the violet heavens. Here and there leaped sudden flame, as some shepherd, feeling lonely, signalled thus to a friend across the plain. Mists rose white and ghost-like; the land seemed turned to silver. The tired children turned to seek their camp to sleep when—

"Lie down!" cried one of the shepherds. "Lie flat on your faces and do not stir! A storm comes!" So urgent was the call that Banda Bela dropped at once flat upon the grass, grasping Marushka's hand and pulling her down beside him.

"Don't be afraid," he said. "Only lie still and the storm will pass above us." She lay like a little frightened bird, trembling and quivering, but saying nothing. The great wind broke over them with a swirl as of fierce waters. It whistled and screamed, blowing with it a fine white dust, then as quickly as it had come it passed, and all was still. Banda Bela raised his head and looked around him. The wind had died down as suddenly as it had sprung up and the plain was so still that not even the grasses stirred. Their shepherd friends rose from the ground where they too had thrown themselves, and one of them called to the children to come back.

"Are you safe?" he asked.

"Oh, yes," said Banda Bela.

"I was frightened, but Banda Bela held my hand," said little Marushka. "Now I am very thirsty."

"The dust and wind always cause great thirst," said the herder. "But no one need be thirsty in the 'Land of a Thousand Springs!' Here is water cool and fresh in the great well, and a little sweet, white wine. Drink and then run quickly away to sleep, for it is late for small men and women."

"What are those giant things which stand so dark against the sky? They frighten me," cried Marushka, as she clung to Banda Bela and looked behind the shepherds' huts.

"Only mighty haystacks, little one. Enough hay is there to last twenty regiments of soldiers fifty years, so that our cattle need never go hungry. Go now. To-morrow you camp here and I will show you many things."

"Would that those children were mine," he said to himself as the two ran away to the camp. "The boy I like, he is clean and straight, and his music stirs my soul; but the little girl reaches my very heart."

CHAPTER III

FROM the Gypsy camp came sounds of wailing. Loud and long the howls arose and Banda Bela sprang from the ground where he had spent the night, to see what was the trouble. He found a group of Gypsies gathered around the door of one of the tents, the women seated on the ground, rocking back and forth, wailing, while the men stood in stolid silence. Then Marushka stole timidly to his side and whispered, "Oh, Banda Bela, old Jarnik is dead. He died in the night." The child's eyes were red with weeping. "They did not know it till the morning. Poor old Jarnik! He was so good and kind!"

Banda Bela looked anxious. Waif and stray that he was he had grown quickly to know his friends from his enemies. Jarnik had been his friend. Now that he was gone would the other Gypsies befriend him? The lonely boy had learned to love little Marushka and hated the thought of leaving her, but he felt that without Jarnik he would not long be welcome in the Gypsy camp. Silently he took the child by the hand and led her away from the wailing crowd of Gypsies.

"We can do no good there, little one," he said. "Come with me. I have a bit of bread from yesterday." Marushka's sobs grew less as he seated her by the roadside and gave her bits of bread to eat.

"Do not cry, little one," he said gently. "Jarnik was old and tired and now he is resting. You must be all mine to care for now. I shall ask Stepan to give you to me." He thought over the last talk he had had with Jarnik.

"Take care of the little one," the old man had said. "She has no one here in all the tribe. She is not a Gypsy, Banda Bela. We found her one day beneath a tall poplar tree beside the road, far, far from here. She could scarcely speak, only lisp her name, ask for 'Mother,' and scold of 'bad Yda.' She was dressed in pretty white clothes and we knew she was the child of rich persons. My daughter had just lost her baby and she begged for the child, so we took her with us. The Gypsies say she will bring bad luck to the tribe, for people say she is stolen, so you must care well for her. There are those in the tribe who wish her ill."

Banda Bela remembered this, and thought how he could protect the little girl from harm. Childlike, her tears soon dry, Maruskha prattled about the sunshine and the sky. As they sat, a huge cloud of dust came down the road. Nearing them, it showed a peasant cart drawn by five fine horses, and in it sat a large peasant woman, broad-bosomed and kindly faced. She smiled as the children stared up at her, and the cart rumbled on and stopped at the shepherds' huts.

Attracted by the gay harness of the horses, the children wandered toward them.

"Good morning, little folk," called out their friend of the night before. "Come and eat again with me. Here is my wife come to spend a few days with me. She has good things in her pockets." Marushka went up to the peasant woman and looked into her face and then climbed into her lap. "I like you," she said, and the woman's arm went around her.

"Poor little dirty thing!" she exclaimed. "I wish I had her at home, Emeric, I would wash and dress her in some of Irma's clothes and she would be as pretty as a wild rose."

"I wash my face every morning," said Marushka, pouting a little. "The other Gypsy children never do." Her dress was open at the neck and showed her little white throat, about which was a string, and the shepherd's wife took hold of it.

"Is it a charm you wear, little one?" she asked.

"No, that is my mother's picture," said Marushka, pulling out of her dress a little silver medal.

"Let me see it." The shepherd's wife examined the bit of silver. "Emeric!" she called to her husband in excited tones. "See here! This is no Gypsy child! Beneath her dress her skin is white—her hair is gold—her eyes are like the sky, and around her neck she wears the medal of Our Lady. She is of Christian parents. She must have been stolen by those thieving Gypsies. What do you know of Marushka?" she demanded, turning to Banda Bela, but the boy only shook his head.

"I have been with the band only a few weeks," he said. "Old Jarnik told me that they found the child deserted by the roadside and took care of her."

"A likely story," sniffed the woman. "I shall go and see this Jarnik!"

"But he cannot answer—" began Banda Bela, when the good woman interrupted—

"Not answer! Boy! there is no man, be he Gypsy or Christian, who will not answer me!" The shepherd nodded his head reminiscently.

"Jarnik won't," said Marushka. "He's dead!"

"Dead!" The woman was a little disconcerted.

"He died during the night," said Banda Bela. "There is great wailing for him now. We came away because nobody wanted us around. They will wail all day."

"Eat with us again, children," said the kind-hearted shepherd. "Your cheeks are the cheeks of famine. You are hungry, both eat! and the boy can make music for us. There will be time enough to question the Gypsies to-morrow."

Before the herder's hut a bough with several short branches protruding from it had been thrust into the ground, and upon these cooking pots had been hung. Soon goulash was simmering in the pot, and kasa was tossed together. The peasant's wife had brought bread and fine cheese, and curious-looking things which the children had never seen before.

"These are potatoes," said she. "They are new things to eat in this part of the country. The Government wants to encourage the people to earn their living from the earth. So it has made a study of all that can be raised in the country. Hungary produces grapes, maize, wheat, cereals, hemp, hops, and all manner of vegetables, and the State helps the people to raise crops in every way that it can. About five years ago the head of the Department of Agriculture decided that the people should be taught to raise potatoes, which are cheap vegetables and very nourishing. Arrangements were made with three large farms at Bars, Nyitra, and Szepes, to raise potatoes from seeds sent them by the Department. The next season these potatoes were distributed for seed to smaller farmers, with the condition that they in turn distribute potatoes for seed to other farmers. In this way nearly everyone soon was raising potatoes.

"Sit and eat," said she, and the children feasted royally. There was white wine to drink, but Marushka had buffalo's milk, cool and sweet. The little girl's face was smiling and she looked bright and happy.

Then Banda Bela played his very best, for the kindness had won his heart.

"Can you sing, boy? Have you music in your throat as well as in your fingers?" asked the shepherd's wife.

"I sing a little, yes," he answered. "I will sing to you the 'Yellow Cockchafer,' which Czuika Panna sang to Ràkoczi."

[Transcriber's Note: You can play this music (MIDI file) by clicking here.]A

Cserebogár sarga cserebogár

Nem Kérdem én töled mi Korlesz nyár

Ast sem Kérdem sokáig élek e?

Csak azt mond meg rozsámé leszek e?

"Little Cockchafer, golden fellow,

I ask thee not when comes the summer time,

Nor do I ask how long shall life be mine.

I ask thee but to tell me

When I my love's shall be."

The boy's voice was sweet and true, and he sang the little song prettily, but so mournfully that tears streamed down the broad, red face of the peasant woman.

"Why do you sing to break one's heart?" she demanded, and Banda Bela answered:

"I sang it but as my mother sang when she was here."

"She is dead, then?"

"She and my father, my brothers and sisters. I have no one left." The boy's face clouded.

"Me you have," said Marushka, with a funny little pout.

"I must go to my herd now," said the shepherd. "Come back to-night and we shall give you your supper for another song."

They reached the shepherd's hut that evening to find his wife awaiting him, but he did not come. He was far away with his herd. As it grew dark his wife gave the children bread and milk and bade them hurry to bed.

"It is late for little children like you," she said. "To-morrow we will see you again. To-day I asked about you at the camp and got but black looks in answer."

Banda Bela hurried Marushka away, fearing a scolding, for he had not meant to stay away all day, but when he reached the camp it was dark and still. The fire was nearly out under the fire-pot, the tent flaps were closed. He dared not waken any one, but Dushka, an old Gypsy woman with an evil face, looked out from her tent.

"Oh, it is you, is it?" she said. "Well, there is no food left, but drink this and you will sleep," and she gave each of the children a mug of dark liquid. It tasted bitter but they drank obediently. Then the old woman took Marushka into her tent while Banda Bela threw himself down under a poplar tree near the fire embers, and was soon fast asleep.

12

CHAPTER IV

DESERTED

BANDA BELA slept heavily through the night. He dreamed in a confused way that he heard the Gypsies talking and one of them said, "She brings ill luck. Men ask of her white locks. The boy is well enough, though one more to feed. But the other brings ill fortune to the band." Another said, "No ill will come to them." Then he dreamed no more, but slept a dead and heavy sleep. He was awakened by a hand upon his shoulder. Some one shook him and he started to his feet to see the shepherd bending over him.

"What is it?" asked Banda Bela.

"Where is your camp and where is the little girl?" demanded the shepherd.

Banda Bela looked around him in amazement. Of the Gypsy camp there was not a trace left, save that dead embers lay where once the fire-pot had been. Tents, carts, horses, Gypsies,— all had vanished from the face of the earth as completely as if they had never been there.

"They have gone and left me!" cried Banda Bela. "Marushka! Where is Marushka?"

"Banda Bela!" called a faint voice behind him, and he turned quickly to see the little girl sitting under a great poplar tree, rubbing her eyes stupidly. He ran to her and the shepherd caught her in his arms.

"What happened in the tent last night?" asked Banda Bela.

"Rosa took me on her lap and cried," said Marushka, "then I went to sleep; but why am I here and where is Rosa?"

"During the night my wife awoke and heard faint sounds of stirring about outside the tent and muffled horses' hoofs. One of the horse herd is missing, many things are taken from the cook hut, and the Gypsies are gone. I do not know why we did not hear them more plainly when they passed," said the shepherd.

"They always tie up their horses' feet in rags when they travel at night," said Banda Bela. "Now they may be many miles from here. No one knows where, for they always cover their tracks. Don't cry, Marushka, I'll take care of you."

"You are but a child yourself," said the shepherd. "Come to my hut and eat and then we shall see what is to be done."

Marushka dried her tears and followed Banda Bela. In silence the two children ate the bread and milk the shepherd's wife prepared for them. Then Banda Bela said:

"Stay here, Marushka. I am going to the cross-roads to see if they have left a sign for us, but I do not think it at all likely."

"What sign would they leave?" asked the shepherd.

"When they go and wish their friends to follow they leave at each cross-road a twig pointing in the direction they have gone. For fear one would think it but a stray twig they cross it with another, and the Gypsy always watches for the crossed branches when following a trail."

"You may look, but you will find no crossed branches at the cross-roads," said the peasant, as Banda Bela ran off. The peasant and his wife talked together in low tones. Soon the boy came back and shook his head mournfully.

"They have left no trail," he said. "They left us behind on purpose."

"The draught they gave you was drugged," said the shepherd. "Tell me, Banda Bela, what will you do?"

"I must take Marushka and go to the city," said the boy. "By walking slowly and often carrying her we can do it. In the city I can play in the streets and earn bread for both."

"But do you like the city? It is noisy and dirty. You will not be free as on the wild," said the peasant's wife.

"I shall like it not at all," said the boy. "But there is nothing else."

"If Marushka will come and live with me I will care for her as my child," said the shepherd's wife. "She shall have clean clothes and plenty to eat and a garden with flowers. Will you come, little one?"

Marushka looked up into the kind face and smiled. "I will come if Banda Bela may come also," she said. The shepherd laughed.

"I told you, Irma, it was useless to take the one without the other. Take both. Banda Bela will serve you well, of that I am sure."

"That I will," said the boy heartily. "Only take care of Marushka and sometimes let me play my music and I will do all that you tell me."

"In this world one can but try," said the shepherd's wife, "then see if good or evil come. I have not the heart to leave these two waifs to starve on this great plain. Come, Emeric, the horses! It will be night before I reach home and there will be much to do."

Almost before the children knew it they found themselves seated beside the shepherd's wife as the cart was whirled along in the opposite direction from which they had come.

They passed country carts made of a huge pine beam with a pair of small wheels at either end. Gay parties of peasants were seated on the pole, the feet braced against a smaller pole.

"What queer-looking people," said Marushka.

"They are not Magyars," said Banda Bela.

"How did you know that?" asked Aszszony Semeyer.

"My father told me many things of Hungary as we travelled together," said the boy. "He told me all the history of how the country first belonged to the Magyars. I remember it almost in the very words he told me."

"What did he say?" demanded Aszszony Semeyer.

"'Many hundreds of years ago the Hungarian people,' he said," began Banda Bela, "'were shepherds who tended their flocks upon the plains of Scythia. The story is that Nimrod, son of Japhet and Enet, his wife, went into the land of Havila, where Enet had two sons, Hunyar and Magyar. These grew up to be strong and to love the chase. One day, as they hunted, they heard sounds of music. These they followed, and came to the hut of the 'Children of the Bush,' where there were two daughters of the king, singing beautifully.

"'Hunyar and Magyar married these two sisters, and their lands were not enough. Westward they moved, from the children of Hunyar coming the Huns, from Magyar's children, the Magyars.

"'They conquered many peoples, but left to each its customs. All were ruled under one chief. So that is why we have so many different peoples to-day.'"

"You know more than I do, Banda Bela," said Aszszony Semeyer.

"My father used to tell me many stories and legends, but I never remembered them very well."

"Marushka, you will be very tired before you reach the village. Curl up on the seat and perhaps you can take a nap."

"Yes, Aszszony," Marushka said obediently, and she and Banda were very quiet.

It was a long drive, but at last the cart rattled down the street of a large village and drew up in front of a white house. Marushka was already asleep and had to be carried into the house. Banda Bela stumbled along after the shepherd's wife and, though with his eyes half shut, obediently ate the bread and milk she put before him. Then he found himself on the kitchen floor before a huge tub of water, with a cake of soap and a large towel.

"Strip! Scrub!" commanded Aszszony Semeyer. "Scrub till you are clean from head to foot, then dry yourself, and I will bring you some clothes. You will never see these again." She picked up a brass tongs from the huge fireplace and with them carried the boy's rags out of the room, her nose fairly curling at the corners with disgust.

Banda Bela did his best. The water was cold, for Hungarians enjoy cold baths, and at the first plunge his teeth chattered. But after a while he rather enjoyed it and scrubbed himself till his dark skin glowed freshly, in spots, it is true, yet he thought it quite wonderful. Not so Aszszony Semeyer. She entered the kitchen, red and flushed with her labours in scouring Marushka.

"You are not clean, no! I will show you—" and she caught up a scrubbing brush. Banda Bela gasped. He would not cry. He was too big a boy for that, but he felt as if he were being ironed with a red-hot iron. Arms, legs, and back,—all were attacked so fiercely that he wondered if there would be any skin left. Half an hour she worked, then wiped him dry and said:

"Now you look like a tame Christian! You are not really clean, it will take many scrubbings to make you that—and more to keep you so—but the worst is done." She cut his wild locks close to his head and surveyed her work proudly.

"Not such a bad-looking boy," she said to herself. "Now for a night shirt and bed." She threw over his head an old cotton shirt and led him up to the attic. "Sleep here," she said, pointing to a clean little bed in one corner. "Rest well and to-morrow we shall see what we can do."

"Where is Marushka?" asked Banda Bela.

"Asleep long ago. You shall see her in the morning," and the boy slept.

The sun woke him early and he lay for a few moments looking about the little room. It was high under the eaves, from which hung long strings of bright red peppers, drying for the winter's use. The morning sun glanced on them and turned them to tongues of fire. From the little window Banda Bela saw down the village street, across the green fields where sparkled rippling brooks, away to the hills. His heart gave a great leap. He had not slept in a room before in all his life. He felt stifled. There was his home, the free, glad föld, he would fly away while yet he could! He sprang from his bed, but where were his rags? Beside his bed was a clean white suit, whole and neat, though patched and mended, and as he paused he heard a voice cry out from below:

"Where is my Banda Bela? I cannot eat my reggeli without Banda Bela."

"I must stay with Marushka," he said to himself, and with a sigh he hurriedly put on the white suit, and ran downstairs. Aszszony Semeyer was in the kitchen.

"Good morning," she said. "One would not know you for the same boy. Marushka is in the garden feeding the geese. Run you and help her," and she pointed to the back of the house, where a little garden was gay with flowers, herbs, and shrubs.

Banda Bela went to find his little charge, but saw only four or five geese and a little peasant girl throwing them handfuls of corn. She was a cute little thing, dressed in a blue skirt, a white waist, and an apron with gaily embroidered stripes. One plait of fair hair hung down her back, while another plait was coiled around her head, pressed low on her brow like a coronet. The child's back was turned toward Banda Bela, and he was about to ask her if she had seen Marushka, when she turned and saw him, and then ran to him, crying,

"Oh, Banda Bela! How nice you look! At first I did not know you, but your eyes are always the same! Haven't I a pretty dress? The shepherd's wife gave it to me. It belonged to her little girl who is dead! Is she not good to us, Banda Bela?"

The boy's sense of gratitude was lively, but the memory of the fearful scrubbing he had received was equally strong within him, and he said:

"She is very good, yes—but, Marushka, did she scrub you last night?"

"Oh, yes, very hard, but I like the feel of myself this morning. Don't I look nice?"

"I should never have known you, and you certainly look nice. I hope you will be happy here."

"Oh, I am very happy," she said, brightly. "Of course I could not be if you were not here, but if you stay with me I shall like it very much. You will stay always, won't you?"

Banda Bela looked across the tiny little garden to the sweep of blue hills beyond the town. They glistened with dew in the morning sun. How fair they looked! But the child's sweet eyes were upon him wistfully and he could not resist their pleading, though the föld and air and sky all called to him and claimed him as their own. He knew how hard it would be for a Gletecore to resist the call of the wander spirit, but to Marushka he said:

"I shall stay with you as long as you need me," and Marushka smiled happily.

"I shall always need you," she said. "So always I shall have you. Now come and see the geese," and she led him to see the white-feathered creatures with whom she had already made friends. There were two big black hairy pigs beside, and from their pen these grunted cheerfully at the children as Aszszony Semeyer called them in to breakfast.

CHAPTER V

THE FAIR OF HAROM-SZÖLÖHOZ

THE village of Harom-Szölöhoz lies on the edge of the plain, where the rolling lands sweep toward the hills and those in turn to the mountains.

Many of the men of the village were sheep or cattle herders, as Emeric Semeyer, living with their herds and seldom returning home save for high days and holidays. Others dwelt in the villages and worked in the grain fields, while still others worked in the salt mines each year for some months at least, for the salt mines of Hungary are famous the world over, and employ many labourers.

It was a pleasant little village. In the centre was an open space around which was clustered the church, with the town house and the larger houses. All the cottages were white-washed, and had gray-shingled roofs. Some of them had gay little flower gardens and a few had trees planted by the doorway. Their shade is not needed, for though the sun is hot, there is always the szöhördo to sit in. This is a seat placed under the eaves which always overhang at one side of the roof. Here often the firewood is stacked and one log serves as a seat upon which the old people may sit and gossip, protected alike from sun and rain.

Upon the doorway of Aszszony Semeyer's house were carved some tulips, a pattern much used in Hungary. In the porch of the house driedkukurut and paprika hung in long ribbons to dry. The front door opened into the kitchen where the soup pot simmered upon the huge brick stove. Many of the cottages in this part of Hungary have but one room, but Aszszony Semeyer was rich and she had two rooms and a loft above. She kept the house wonderfully clean, yet she always seemed to have plenty of time to sit at the window and embroider varrotas. The varrotas are Hungarian embroideries worked with red and black and blue threads upon linen cloth the colour of pale ochre. The thread and linen is woven by the women, and in nearly every cottage in the village some one may be seen seated at the window spinning, weaving, or embroidering.

Aszszony Semeyer's father had been one of the beres employed by the Tablabiro, and he had been able to leave his daughter, for he had no sons, a cottage and some money, so that she was better off than many of the village people. This did not keep her from working hard, for all Magyars are industrious and hard working. She did not intend that any one under her care should be idle; and Banda Bela found that he and Marushka must work if they were to eat.

WASHING IN THE RIVER

"Now then, my sugars," she said to them, "we shall see what there is for you to do! Some work there must be for one and the other. But a square pane will not fit a round window, so we must give you something that you can do out of doors. You, Banda Bela, shall go to help the swine-herd, and Marushka shall be goose girl."

"Oh, I should like that!" cried Marushka. "I think the geese are so funny and I like to see them eat."

"You shall learn to embroider, and, as you sit on the meadow watching the geese, you can place many stitches. When you marry you will have whole chests full of embroideries, like any well brought up maiden. Otherwise you will be shamed before your husband's people.

"Banda Bela, you shall go with the swine-herd. That will keep you out of doors, and you will like that, I am sure."

"I will try," said Banda Bela. "But I have never worked."

"Quite time you learned, then," said the good woman. "We will start in the morning. To-day you and Marushka may go about the village and make yourselves at home. You will find much to interest you. Come back when the big bell of the church rings. That will be dinner time."

"Oh, Banda Bela, see those people jumping up and down in the river!" said Marushka. "What are they doing?"

"Washing, I think," said Banda Bela. "See, they take a dress or an apron and put it in the stream and tread on it, stamping it against the stones until the dirt all comes out, then they rinse it out and put it in their wooden trays and take another piece and wash it."

"I thought the wooden trays were cradles for babies," said Marushka. "The Gypsies use them for that."

"Yes, but I have seen them used for many things," said Banda Bela. "The peasants carry goods to market in them; in the city the baker boys use them to carry bread, washwomen use them, and cooks use them to cut up meat for goulash or to chop paprika in."

"Banda Bela, we're coming to such a crowded place,—what are all those people doing?" asked Marushka, pointing to a street which was crowded to overflowing with peasants, their white costumes and gay aprons and jackets flashing about like bright birds in the sunlight.

"It must be a market day," said the boy. "I have often seen the village markets when I was travelling with my father. It might be fair time, and that is great fun! Let us go and see, Marushka. They have lots of pretty things in the stalls."

The two children ran down the street, which was filled with carts, covered with gay-coloured cloths, the horses having been taken out and stabled elsewhere.

Stalls had been built up and down the sides of the street and these were filled with fruit, melons, embroidery, clothes, and wonderful crockery. Plates and jugs in gay colours and artistic designs have been made by the peasants in this part of Hungary for hundreds of years, and in the cottages one can see, hung along the walls under the rafters, jugs, cups, and platters of great beauty. No peasant would part with his family china, as he would feel disgraced unless he could display it up on his walls.

Ox carts lumbered down the streets, the huge horns of the oxen frightening Marushka. Boys with huge hats, loose white shirts, and trousers above the ankles, bare-footed girls and girls in top boots, men and women, geese, pigs, horses, and cows, all crowded into the square, where were the church with its white spire and golden cross, the magistrate's house, and the inn named "Harom Szölöhoz" as its three bunches of grapes above the door showed.

"Banda Bela," said Marushka, "what are those women sitting behind those red and yellow pots for? They look so funny with the great flat hats on their heads."

"They are cooking," said Banda Bela. "I have seen these village fairs when I used to travel with my father. In the bottom of those pots is burning charcoal upon which a dish is set. In the dish they cook all kinds of things, frying meat in bacon fat, making goulash and anything else a customer may want."

"Isn't that funny!" said Marushka, whose idea of cookery was the Gypsy fire-pot over a fire of sticks. "What lovely frocks the girls wear! I like those boots with the bright red tops, too,—I wish I had some," and she looked down discontentedly at her ten little bare toes. Banda Bela laughed at her.

"You're a funny little bit of a Marushka," he said. "Yesterday you hadn't a frock to your name, only a little rag of a shirt, and you were all dirty and your hair had never been combed. Now you have a pretty dress and an embroidered apron, and hair like a high-born princess, yet you are not satisfied, but must have top boots! They would pinch and hurt your feet terribly and cramp your toes so that you couldn't wiggle them at all. After you had worn boots awhile your toes would get so stiff that you couldn't use them as fingers as we do. People who always wear boots cannot even pick up anything with their toes. If they want a stick or anything that has fallen to the ground they have to bend the back and stoop to pick it up with the fingers."

Marushka looked thoughtful for a moment, her little toes curling and wriggling as she dug them into the sand, then she said:

"But the boots are so pretty, Banda Bela, I would like them!" The boy laughed.

"You will have to have them someway, little sister," he said. "And one of those bright little jackets, too, since you so much like to be dressed up like a fine bird."

"Why do some of the women wear jackets and some not, and some of them such queer things on their heads?" asked Marushka.

"This fair brings people from all around and there are many kinds of people in Hungary," he said. "Those tall straight men with faces all shaved except for the waxed moustache are Magyars, while the fair-haired fellows who look as if they didn't care about their clothes and slouch around are called Slövaks. The girls who wear those long, embroidered, white robes, sandals on their feet and black kerchiefs on their heads, are Roumanians. The Magyar girls wear gold-embroidered aprons, big white sleeves and zouave jackets, and the boots you like so much."

"I am a Magyar," said Marushka, tossing her head proudly. "All but the boots."

"High-born Princess, boots you shall have," laughed Banda Bela. "But how?" He knit his brows, as they stopped at a stall where boots were displayed for sale. "I know!" he cried, while Marushka looked longingly at the boots. "I shall play for them."

His violin was under his arm, and he raised it to his chin, tuned it softly, and quickly began a little tune. Hungarians love music and it was but a moment before a crowd gathered around. He played a gay little song, "Nezz roysám a szemembe," one of the old Magyar love songs in which a lover implores his sweetheart to look into his eyes and read there that for him she shines like a star in the blue of heaven, and when he had finished everyone cried for more. This time he whisked into a dance tune and feet patted in time to the music and faces were fairly wreathed in smiles. When he stopped with a gay flourish, everybody cried, "More, boy, more!" and Banda Bela smiled happily as one in the crowd tossed him a krajczar. He took off his cap and passed it around among the crowd. Many a krajczar fell into it and one silver piece came from a Magyar officer, a tall fine-looking man with a sad face, who stood on the edge of the crowd.

"Who are you, boy, and why do you play? Do you need money?" asked the officer.

"Not for myself, Your Gracious Highness, but the little one wishes red-topped boots and also a jacket," said the boy simply.

"These of course she must have," said the officer, with a smile which lighted up his sad face. "Where is this little sister of yours? At home with her mother?"

"No, Most High-Born Baron," said Banda Bela. "The mother I have not, but Aszszony Semeyer is very kind to us, and Marushka is here with me. That little maid by the cooking stall."

"She is a fair little maid, of course she must have her boots," said the officer. "But you have earned them, for your music is like wine to empty hearts. What is your name, boy, and where do you live?"

"My name is Banda Bela, Most Gracious Baron. I live since yesterday at the house of Emeric Semeyer. My father was Gergeley Banda, the musician, now dead."

"I have often seen and heard your father in Buda-Pest," said the officer kindly, laying his hand on the boy's shoulder. "You will play as well as he did if you keep on."

Banda Bela's eyes shone.

"That would please me more than anything else in all the world," he said. "I think now I have enough for Marushka's boots, so I need not play more, save one thing for the pleasure of those who have paid me. I will play a song of my fathers," and he played a gentle little melody, with a sad, haunting strain running through it, which brought tears to the eyes.

"Boy, you are a genius! What is that?" asked the baron when he had finished.

"It is called the 'Lost One,'" said Banda Bela. "The little song running through it is of a child who has been lost from home. The words are:

"The hills are so blue,

The sun so warm,

The wind of the moor so soft and so kind!

Oh, the eyes of my mother,

The warmth of her breast,

The breath of her kiss on my cheek, alas!"

The officer put a whole silver dollar in the boy's hand and turned away without a word, and Banda Bela wondered as he saw tears in the stern eyes.

Then Marushka got her boots and her jacket and Banda Bela bought some new strings for his violin, and a little box of sugar jelly which he took to Aszszony Semeyer, and to her also he gave the store of krajczar left after his purchases had been made.

20

CHAPTER VI

VILLAGE LIFE

BANDA BELA found life with the pigs rather quiet in spite of the noise his four-footed friends made, but he soon learned to know all the pigs by name and to like them, dirty as they were, but he never grew fond of them as Marushka did of the village geese. These followed her like a great white army, as she led them beside the river. They seemed to understand every word she said and would squawk in answer to her call, and come with flapping wings across the field, whenever she spoke to them.

So, too, would the storks who nested in the eaves of the houses, and it was a funny sight to see the long-legged, top-heavy birds stalking around after Marushka, until she gave them bits of her black bread, when they would spread their great wings and fly off contentedly to their nestlings in the eaves.

Marushka's hours at home were quite as busy as those she spent with the geese, for Aszszony Semeyer was a noted housekeeper and did not intend that any little girl under her care should grow up without learning to do housework. Marushka learned to embroider, to sew, to mend, to clean the floors and to cook. She was an apt pupil and it was not long before she could cook even turoscsusza as well as her teacher. Turoscsusza is not easy to make. First one mixes a paste of rye and barley meal, stirred up with salt and water. This is rolled out thin and cut into little squares which are dropped quickly into boiling water, then taken out, drained and put into a hot frying pan, with some curds and fried bacon, and cooked over a hot fire. It takes practice to know just how long it must be cooked to make it to perfection, and Marushka felt very much encouraged when Aszszony Semeyer said to her at last:

"You can make it just as well as I can, child." The little girl knew that no higher compliment could be paid her.

At Christmas time she learned to make the hazel-nut cakes which are so deliciously good, and she and Banda Bela enjoyed the Christmas tree, the first they had ever seen, and which is found in every peasant household in Hungary. In the poorer cottages it is often but a little fir branch decorated with bits of coloured tissue paper and a few candles, but Aszszony Semeyer had a large tree, with all sorts of decorations and presents for the children, who got up at five o'clock to see them, though Marushka was very sleepy, for she had stayed up for the midnight Mass on Christmas Eve. Banda Bela had first helped Aszszony Semeyer "strew the straw," one of the quaint Christmas customs in this part of Hungary, where the peasants strew fresh straw upon the floor and sit upon it to insure their hens laying plenty of eggs during the coming year. He also made up the "plenty brush," taking an onion for Aszszony Semeyer, Marushka, and himself, with little bundles of hay and barley ears tied with scarlet ribbon and laid upon the table. This will be sure to bring plenty of onions, hay, and barley to the house during the year.

In order to keep off fire Banda Bela and Marushka had each taken some beans on a plate and raced all around the szvoba, touching the wall with the plate, and they had given the pigs and the geese bits of salt to bring them good luck.

Thus the winter passed busily and pleasantly for the two children. They lived on simple but hearty fare. For breakfast there was czibere, made by steeping black bread in water for three weeks until it soured, and making this into soup by adding beaten eggs and sheep's milk. For dinner they had often goulash or turoscsusza with vegetables or bread.

Marushka learned also to boil soap, to make candles, dry prunes, and smoke sausages. She helped to cure the hams, crying bitterly over the death of Banda Bela's little piggies. She churned and made cheese, much of which was stored up for winter use, as were also many of the vegetables from the little garden, which Banda Bela weeded and cared for.

Both children helped to make the slivovitza, or plum brandy, of which every Hungarian household must have some, and which is very good to drink.

Right after Easter the children were invited to a wedding, and as Banda Bela was to play for the czardas, Marushka was delighted.

One of the neighbours, just at the end of the village, had several élado leanyök, called this because in Hungary a bridegroom must pay his father-in-law a good price if he wishes a wife. Sometimes a peasant pays only twenty florins for his wife, but sometimes he has to pay as much as two hundred florins.

The day before Irma's marriage, Lajos, the best man, came to the door of Aszszony Semeyer's cottage. Bowing and taking off his hat, he said:

"Most humbly do I beg your pardon for my intrusion under your roof, but I am deputed to politely invite you and your family to partake of a morsel of food and drink a glass of wine, and to dance a measure thereafter on the occasion of the wedding feast of the seed that has grown up under their wings. Please bring with you knives, forks, and plates."

Aszszony Semeyer accepted the invitation, and as Sömögyi Irma was a Slövak girl, the marriage ceremonies were very different from those which a Magyar maiden would have had.

The Slövak wedding is all arranged for by the best man. Of course the young people have been lovers for some time and have plighted their troth through the window on a moonlight night, but no one is supposed to know about that. The lover and his friend, who is called the staro sta, on a Saturday night go to the door of the lady's cottage and say:

"Good friends, we have lost our way. In the king's behalf we seek a star." At this the girl hastily leaves the room and the staro sta exclaims:

"Behold! There is the star for which we seek. May we go and seek her? We have flowers with us to deck her, flowers fair as those which Adam bound upon the brow of Eve in the Garden."

"I will call her back," says the bride's father, and the girl returns to smilingly accept the staro sta's flowers, and his offer of marriage for his friend. The flowers are distributed, speeches are made, and everybody drinks the health of the betrothed pair in slivovitza, binding their hands together with a handkerchief.

The night before the wedding there is a cake dance, when the czardas is danced, the wedding cake is displayed, and everybody cries, laughs, and puts a bit of money into a plate to help toward the wedding expenses, for the wedding feast must last two days, and it costs a great deal of money.

Irma's feast was very fine, for her father was village magistrate and could afford to make her marriage quite a social event. Even the High-Born Baron and Baroness from the great house came, and Marushka was delighted to see them, for she had heard the little peasant girls tell how kind the Baron was, and how beautiful his wife.

The High-Born Baron danced the czardas with the bride and the High-Born Baroness trod the measures with the bridegroom, and Marushka could hardly keep her eyes off the Baroness. Her eyes were soft and brown, her teeth white as little pearls, her complexion a soft olive with rose-hued cheeks, her hair blue-black, soft and fine, waving about her face and piled high with roses at each side above her ears. Her dress was of brocaded silk, the bodice trimmed with pearls, the large sleeves filmy with laces almost as fine as those she might have worn to court. Hungarian women love fine clothes and dress beautifully and the High-Born Baroness wished to pay honor to Sömögyi Vazul, for he had served the Baron's house and his father's before him.

The Baron wore his handsomest uniform, top boots, embroidered coat and magnificent cloak, trimmed in gold braid and buttons, and it was a proud moment in Irma's life when he put his hand upon her elbow and led her out to dance the quaint dance of the Hungarians, with its slow movement gradually growing faster and faster until it ends in a regular whirl.

Banda Bela played his best and the czardas of Irma's wedding was long talked of in the village as the most beautiful which had ever been danced. Then the High-Born Baron spoke to his wife and she smiled and nodded her head and asked Banda Bela if he could play the accompaniment to any of the folk-songs.

"Yes, Your Graciousness," he answered, "to any one of them."

"Then I will sing for you," said the Baroness, and a rustle of expectancy went round the 'szvoba, for it was well known in the village that the High-Born Graciousness was a famous singer and had often been asked to sing to the King. She sang the little folk-song which every Hungarian knows.

"How late the summer stars arise!

My love for thee was late in rising too.

But what of that, or aught, to me?

Why is thy glance so icy cold?

My heart burns hot with love for thee!"

Her voice was tender and sad like that of all the Magyar women, and Marushka thought she had never heard anything so beautiful as the song to which Banda Bela's notes added a perfect accompaniment.

Then the wedding cakes were passed about, and the little girl had her full share. Banda Bela rejoiced in the present of a silver piece from the Baron.

"Who is this child?" demanded the Baroness, attracted by Marushka's fair hair amidst the dark-haired little Magyars and Slövaks.

"A little one adopted by Aszszony Semeyer," replied the magistrate, "as is also the Gypsy boy who played for you."

"She does not look like a Gypsy child," said the Baroness, knitting her brows a little. "She reminds me of some one I have seen—" as Marushka smiled up at her and made her a quaint little peasant's courtesy with more than peasant's grace.

23

CHAPTER VII

THE UNEXPECTED

ASZSZONY SEMEYER'S brother-in-law had a large vineyard and, when it came time for the vintage, the good woman drove the children over to her brother's farm. The grapes grew in long lines up and down the hillside where the sun was strongest. White carts, drawn by white oxen, were driven by white-frocked peasants. All were decked with grape leaves, all had eaten golden grapes until they could eat no more, for the great bunches of rich, yellow grapes are free to all at vintage time. From these golden grapes is made the amber-hued "Riesling," and the children enjoyed very much helping to tread the grapes, for the wine is made in the old-fashioned way, the grapes being cast into huge vats and trod upon with the feet till the juice is entirely pressed out. The peasants dance gaily up and down upon the grapes, tossing their arms above their heads and making great pleasure of their work.

After the long, happy, sunny day the white cart of Aszszony Semeyer joined the line of carts which wound along from the vineyard, filled with gay toilers. At her brother's farm they stayed all night, for the vintage dance upon the grass under the golden glow of the harvest moon was too fair a sight to miss.

They stayed, too, for the nut-gathering. Hungarian hazel nuts are celebrated the world over, and the nutting was as much a fête as had been the vintage. This was the last frolic of the year, and the children went back to Harom Szölöhoz to work hard all winter. Banda Bela still helped the swine-herd, but Marushka was no longer a goose girl. Aszszony Semeyer had grown very fond of the little girl and spent long hours teaching her to sew and embroider. Many salt tears little Marushka shed over her Himmelbelt, or marriage bed-cover. Every girl in Hungary is supposed to have a fine linen bedspread embroidered ready to take to her home when she is married. It takes many months to make one of them, and Marushka's was to be a very elaborate one.

The linen was coarse, but spun from their own flax by Aszszony Semeyer herself. In design Marushka's Himmelbelt was wonderful. The edge was to be heavily embroidered in colours, and in one corner was Marushka's name, a space being left for the day of the wedding. In the centre was a wedding hymn which was embroidered in gay letters, and began:

"Blessed by the Saints and God above I'll be

If I do wed the man who loveth me;

Then may my home be full of peace and rest,

And I with goodly sons and daughters blest!"

Marushka worked over it for hours and grew to fairly hate the thought of marrying.

"I shall never, never marry," she sobbed. "I shall never finish this horrid old Himmelbelt and I suppose I can't be married without it."

Banda Bela sympathized with her and often played for her while she worked. Through the long winter the children learned to read and write, for all children are compelled to go to school in Hungary, and the Gypsies are the only ones who escape the school room.

Marushka learned very fast. Her mind worked far more quickly than did Banda Bela's, though he was so much older. There was nothing which Marushka did not want to know all about; earth, air, sky, water, sun, wind, people,—all were interesting to her.

"The wind, Banda Bela, whence comes it?" she would ask.

"It is the breath of God," the boy would answer.

"And the sun?"

"It is God's kindness."

"But the storms, with the flashing lightning and the terrible thunder?"

"It is the wrath of Isten, the flash of his eye, the sound of his voice."

"But I like to know what makes the things," said Marushka. "It is not enough to say that everything is God. I know He is back of everything. Aszszony Semeyer told me that, but I want to know the how of what He does."

"I think we cannot always do just what we like," said Banda Bela calmly. "I have found that out many times, so it is best not to fret about things but to live each day by itself." At this philosophy Marushka pouted.

One afternoon in the summer the children asked for permission to go to the woods, and Aszszony Semeyer answered them:

"Yes, my pigeons, go; the sky is fair and you have both been good children of late,—go, but return early."

They had a happy afternoon playing together upon the hills which were so blue with forget-me-nots that one could hardly see where the hilltops met the sky. Marushka made a wreath of them and Banda Bela crowned her, twining long festoons of the flowers around her neck and waist, until she looked like a little flower fairy. They wandered homeward as the sun was setting, past the great house on the hill, and Maruskha said:

"I wonder if the High-Born Baron and his gracious lady will soon be coming home? In the village they say that they always come at this time of the year. Do you remember how beautiful the High-Born Baroness looked at Irma's wedding?"

"She was beautiful and kind, and sang like a nightingale," said Banda Bela. "Come, Marushka, we must hurry, or Aszszony Semeyer will scold us for being late!"

As they neared the village they heard a noise and a strange scene met their gaze! A yoke of white oxen blocked the way; several black and brown cattle had slipped their halters and were running aimlessly about tossing their horns; seventeen hairy pigs ran hither and thither, squealing loudly, and all the geese in town seemed to be turned loose, flapping their wings and squawking at the top of their voices. Children were dashing around, shouting and screaming, in their efforts to catch the different animals, while the grown people, scarcely less disturbed, tried in vain to silence the din.

"They are frightened by the machine of the High-Born Baron, Marushka," said Banda Bela. "See, there it is at the end of the street. I have seen these queer cars in Buda-Pest, but none has ever been in this little village before, so it is no wonder that everyone is afraid. There, the men have the cattle quiet, but the geese and the pigs are as bad as ever."

"Let us run and lead them out, Banda Bela," cried Marushka. "You can make the pigs follow you and I can quiet the geese. It is too bad to have the homecoming of their High-Born Graciousnesses spoiled by these stupids!" Marushka dashed into the throng of geese calling to them in soft little tones. They recognized her at once and stopped their fluttering as she called them by the names she had given them when she was goose girl and they all flocked about her. Then she sang a queer little crooning song, and they followed her down the street as she walked toward the goose green, not knowing how else to get them out of the way.

Banda Bela meantime was having an amusing time with his friends the pigs. They were all squealing so loudly that they could scarcely hear his voice, so he bethought himself of his music and began to play. It was but a few moments before the piggies heard and stopped to listen. Banda Bela had played much when he was watching the pigs on the moor, and his violin told them of the fair green meadow where they found such good things to eat, and of the river's brink with its great pools of black slime in which to wallow. They stopped their mad dashing about and gathered around the boy, and he, too, turned and led them from the village.

It was a funny sight, this village procession. First came Marushka in her little peasant's costume, decked with her wreath and garlands of forget-me-nots, and followed by her snow-white geese. Next, Banda Bela, playing his violin and escorting his pigs, while last of all came the motor car of the High-Born Baron, the Baron looking amused, the Baroness in spasms of laughter.

"Oh, Léon," she cried. "Could our friends who drive on the Os Budavara see us now! Such a procession! That child who leads is the most beautiful little creature and so unconscious, and the boy's playing is wonderful."

"FIRST CAME MARUSHKA"

"They must be the Gypsy children Aszszony Semeyer adopted. We saw them when we were here last year," replied her husband. "What a story this would make for the club! We must give these children a florin for their timely aid."

But the children, unconscious of this pleasant prospect, led their respective friends back into the village by another way, so that it was not until the next day that the "High-Born" ones had a chance to see them, and this time in an even more exciting adventure than that of the village procession. It was the motor car again which caused the trouble.

Marushka and Banda Bela had been sent on an errand to a farm not far from the village and were walking homeward in the twilight. Down the road came a peasant's cart just as from the opposite direction came the "honk-honk" of the Baron's motor. Such a sight had never appeared to the horses before in all their lives. They reared up on their hind legs, pawing the air wildly as the driver tried to turn them aside to let the motor pass. A woman and a baby sat in the cart, and, as the horses became unmanageable and overturned the cart into the ditch, the woman was thrown out and the baby rolled from her arms right in front of the motor. The mechanician had tried to stop his car, but there was something wrong with the brake and he could not stop all at once. Marushka saw the baby. If there was one thing she loved more than another it was a baby. She saw its danger and in a second she dashed across the road, snatched up the little one and ran up the other side of the road just as the motor passed over the spot where the baby had fallen.

"Marushka," cried Banda Bela as he ran around the motor. "Are you hurt?"

"Brave child!" cried the Baron, who sprang from his car and hurried to the group of frightened peasants. "Are you injured?"

"Not at all, Most Noble Baron," said Marushka, not forgetting to make her courtesy, though it was not easy with the baby in her arms.

The child's mother had by this time picked herself out of the ditch and rushed over to where Maruskha stood, the baby still in her arms and cooing delightedly as he looked into the child's sweet face, his tiny hand clutching the silver medal which always hung about Marushka's neck. The mother snatched the baby to her breast and, seating herself by the roadside, she felt all over its little body to see if it was hurt.

"You have this brave little girl to thank that your baby was not killed," said the Baron. The woman turned to Marushka.

"I thank you for—" she began, stopped abruptly, and then stared at the little girl with an expression of amazement. "Child, who are you?" she demanded.

"Marushka," said the little girl simply. The woman put her hand to her head.

"It is her image," she muttered. "Her very self!"

The Baroness had alighted from the motor and came up in time to hear the woman's words.

"Whose image?" she demanded sharply.

The woman changed colour and put her baby down on the grass.

"The little girl looks like a child I saw in America," she stammered, her face flushing.

"Was she an American child?" demanded the Baroness.

"Oh, yes, Your Graciousness," said the woman hastily. "Of course, she was an American child."

"Now I know that you are speaking falsely," said the Baroness. "This little one looks like no American child who was ever born. Léon," turning to her husband, "is this one of your peasants?" Then she added in a tone too low to be heard by anyone but her husband, "I know that she can tell something about this little girl. Question her."

The Baron turned to the woman and said:

"This little girl saved your baby's life. Should you not do her some kindness?"

"What could I do for her, Your High-Born Graciousness?" the woman asked.

"That I leave to your good heart." The Baron had not dwelt upon his estates and managed his peasants for years without knowing peasant character. Threats would not move this woman, that he saw in a moment.

"She is a Gypsy child," the woman said sullenly.

Banda Bela spoke suddenly, for he had come close and heard what was said.

"That she is not! She is Magyar. Deserted by the roadside, she was cared for by Gypsy folk. Does she look like a Gypsy? Would a Gypsy child wear a Christian medal upon her breast?" The boy's tone was sharp. Marushka heard nothing. She was playing with the baby.

The woman looked from Marushka to the baby, then at the Baron, hesitating. "Let me see your pretty medal, child," she said at length, and Marushka untied the string and put the medal in the woman's hand.

"I used to think it was my mother, but now I know it is Our Lady," said Marushka gently. The woman looked at it for a moment, then gave it back to the little girl and stood for a moment thinking.

"High-Born Baron," she said at last, "I will speak. Those it might harm are dead. The little girl who saved my baby I will gladly serve, but I will speak alone to the ears of the Baron and his gracious lady."

"Very well," said the Baron as he led the woman aside.

"Škultéty Yda is my name, Your Graciousness," she said. "I was foster-sister to a high-born lady in the Province in which lies Buda-Pest. I loved my mistress and after her marriage I went with her to the home of her husband, a country place on the Danube. There I met Hödza

Ludevit, who wished to marry me and take me to America, for which he had long saved the money. He hated all nobles and most of all the High-Born Count, because the Count had once struck him with his riding whip. Then the Countess' little daughter came and I loved her so dearly that I said that I would never part from her. Ludevit waited for me two years, then he grew angry and said, 'To America I will go with or without you.' Then he stole the little baby and sent me word that he would return her only on condition that I go at once to America with him. To save the little golden-haired baby I followed him beyond the sea to America. He swore to me that he had returned little Marushka to her parents.

"The Count traced us to America thinking we might have taken the child with us, and then I learned that the baby had never been sent home. My wicked husband had left it by the roadside and what had become of it no one knew. It turned my heart toward my husband into stone. Now he is dead and I have brought my own baby home, but my family are all dead and I have no place to go. These people were kind to me on the ship, so I came to them, hoping to find work to care for my baby, since all my money was spent in the coming home. This little girl who saved my baby I know to be the daughter of my dear mistress." She stopped.

"How do you know it?" demanded the Baroness.

"Your High-Born Graciousness, she is her image. There is the same corn-coloured hair, the same blue eyes, the same flushed cheek, the same proud mouth, the same sweet voice."

"What was the name of your lady?" interrupted the baroness, who had been looking fixedly at Marushka, knitting her brows. "The child has always reminded me of someone; who it is I cannot think."

"The foster sister whom I loved was the Countess Maria Andrássy."

"I see it," cried the Baroness. "The child is her image, Léon. I have her picture at the castle. You will see at once the resemblance. I have not seen Maria since we left school. Her husband we see often at Court. I had heard that Maria had lost her child and that since she had never left her country home. I supposed the child was dead. This little Marushka must be Maria Andrássy."

"We must have proofs," said the Baron.

"Behold the medal upon the child's neck," said Yda. "It is one her mother placed there. I myself scratched with a needle the child's initials 'M. A.' the same as her mother's. The letters are still there; and if that is not enough there is on the child's neck the same red mark as when she was born. It is up under her hair and her mother would know it at once."

"The only way is for her mother to see her and she will know. This Gypsy boy may be able to supply some missing links. We shall ask him," said the Baron. When Banda Bela was called he told simply all that he knew about Marushka and all that old Jarnik had told him.

"There is no harm coming to her, is there?" he asked anxiously, and the Baroness said kindly:

"No, my boy, no harm at all, and perhaps much good, for we think that we have found her people." Banda Bela's face clouded. "That would make you sad?" she asked.

"Yes and no, Your Graciousness," he answered. "It would take my heart away to lose Marushka for whom I have cared these years as my sister, but I know so well the sadness of having no mother. If she can find her mother, I shall rejoice."

"Something good shall be found for you, too, my lad." The Baroness smiled at him, but he replied simply:

"I thank Your High-Born Graciousness. I shall still have my music."

The Baroness flashed a quick glance at him. "I understand you, boy; nothing can take that away from one who loves it. Now take the little one home, and to-morrow we shall come to see Aszszony Semeyer about her. In the meantime, say not one word to the little girl for fear she be disappointed if we have made a mistake."

"Yes, Your High-Born Graciousness," and Banda Bela led Marushka away, playing as they went down the hill the little song of his father.

"The hills are so blue,

The sun so warm,

The wind of the moor so soft and so kind!

Oh, the eyes of my mother,

The warmth of her breast,

The breath of her kiss on my cheek, alas!"

CHAPTER VIII

MARUSHKA MAKES A JOURNEY

MARUSHKA was so excited that she scarce knew how to contain herself. The Baroness had come to see Aszszony Semeyer and had talked long with her. Then she had called Marushka and the little girl saw that Aszszony Semeyer had been crying.

"Marushka," the Baroness said. "Will you come with me and make a journey? I want to take you in the motor to Buda-Pest."

"The High-Born Baroness is very good," said Marushka, her eyes shining. "I should like to go very much, but not if Aszszony Semeyer does not wish it."

"Good child," said Aszszony Semeyer, "I do wish it."

"Then why do you cry?"

"There are many things to make old people cry," said the peasant woman. "I am certainly not crying because the High-Born Graciousness wishes to honour you with so pleasant a journey—(that is the truth, for it is the fear that she will not come back that forces the tears from my eyes," she added to herself).

"Aszszony Semeyer will have Banda Bela," said the Baroness. Marushka opened her eyes very wide.

"Oh, no, Your Graciousness, because Banda Bela must go wherever I go. If he stays at home, then I must stay, too."

"Such a child!" exclaimed Aszszony Semeyer. "She has always been like this about Banda Bela. The two will not be separated."

"In that case we shall have to take Banda Bela also," said the Baroness, and Marushka clapped her hands with glee.

"That will be nice," she exclaimed. "I shall love to see the city and all the beautiful palaces, and I shall bring you a present, Aszszony Semeyer, but I will not go unless you wish me to."

"I do wish it, dear child, but do not forget your old aunt," for so she had taught the children to call her.

So it was decided that they should start the next week when the Baron's business would have been attended to.

Part of Marushka's journey was to be taken in the motor, and, as she had never ridden in one before, she was very much excited as they set out on a bright day in August. She wanted to sit beside Banda Bela with the driver, but the Baroness said, "No, it would not be proper for a little girl." So she had to be satisfied with sitting between the Baron and Baroness on the back seat.

Up hill and down dale they rode. The road at times was so poor that the wheels wedged in the ruts and all had to get out while the driver pushed from behind.

They ate their luncheon at a ruined castle which had once been a beautiful country place. It belonged to a friend of the Baron but had been deserted for many years. Beyond it lay a corn-coloured plain and blue hills, and on top of one of the hills gleamed the white walls of a monastery.

"Near here are some famous marble quarries," said the Baroness. "They are finer even than the ones at Carrara in Italy, which are celebrated all over the world. There is so much marble around here that it is cheaper than wood. See there! even the walls of that pig-pen are of marble. Yonder is a peasant's hut with a marble railing around the garden. Even the roads are mended with it, and the quarries in the hillsides have hardly been touched yet. Some day someone will be made very rich if they will open up this industry, and it will keep many of our people from going to America."

"Why do they go to America?" asked Marushka. "And where is America? It cannot be so nice as Magyarland."

"Well, little one, it is as nice to Americans, but when our Hungarian people go there they always come back. Sometimes the Slövaks remain, but never the Magyars. They go there and work and save. Then they send for their families, and they too work and save, and at last they all come home. There is a story told of the last war in Hungary. Two Magyar peasants had gone to America and worked in the far west. One day in a lonely cabin on the plains they found an old newspaper and read that there was war in Hungary. They put together all their money, saved and scrimped, ate little and worked hard, until they got enough to go home. They reached Hungary before the fighting was over and begged to be sent at once to the front, to have a chance to serve their country before the war was over."

"But how do people know about America?" asked Marushka.

"There are agents of the steamship companies who go from village to village trying to get the people to emigrate," said the Baroness. "They tell them that in America one finds gold rolling about in the streets and that there everyone is free and equal. Our people believe it and go there. Many of those who go are bad and discontented or lazy here at home. When they get to America and find that gold does not roll in the streets and that they must work for it if they want it, they are more discontented than ever, and the people of America think that Hungarians are lazy and good for nothing. When they come home they talk in the villages of the grand things they did in America and make the people here discontented and unhappy."

"Why don't the people ask them, if America was so nice, why did they not stay there?" asked Marushka, and the Baroness smiled.

"Those of us who have estates to take care of wish they would," she said. "The returned emigrant is one of the problems of Hungary."

"Why are there so many beggars?" asked Marushka. "I never saw one in Harom Szölöhoz."

"That is a prosperous village with a kind over-lord," said the Baroness. "But there are so many beggars in Hungary that they have formed themselves into a kind of union. In some towns there is a beggar chief who is as much a king in his way as is His Majesty the Emperor. The chief has the right to say just where each beggar may beg and on what days they may beg in certain places. The beggars never go to each other's begging places, and if anyone does, the other beggars tell the police about him and he is driven out of town.

"In some provinces the very old and sick people are sent to live with the richest householders. Of course no one would ever refuse to have them, for alms asked in the name of Christ can never be refused, and as our gracious Emperor has said, 'Sorrow and suffering have their privileges as well as rank.'"

"He must be a very good Emperor," said Marushka. "It seems to me that you are a very wonderful lady and that you know everything. It is interesting to know all about these things. When I grow up I am going to know all about Magyarland."

The journey in the train was even more exciting for the children than that in the motor, and they enjoyed very much hearing about the various places through which they passed.

When they reached Buda-Pest, Marushka was dumbfounded, for she had never imagined anything so beautiful. The train rolled into the huge station, with its immense steel shed and glass roof, upon which the sun beat like moulten fire. The children followed the Baroness through the gate and into the carriage, which rattled away so quickly that it swayed from side to side, for in Hungary people are proudof their fine horses and always drive as fast as they can.

Marushka caught glimpses of broad, well-paved streets and large, handsome buildings, as the Baroness pointed out the opera house, theatres, churches, museums, and the superb houses of parliament built upon the banks of the Danube.

"Across the river you see Buda," said the Baroness. "In old times Buda was very old-fashioned, but in the last twenty years the royal palace has been built and many other costly buildings, and soon it will be as handsome as Pest. The improvements within the last ten years are wonderful. The streets are clean and neat, no ugly signs are permitted upon the houses, no refuse on the streets, and the citizens vie with each other in trying to make that side of the river as beautiful as this. The Emperor takes great interest in the enterprise."

"You speak about the Emperor sometimes," said Marushka. "And other times about the King. Who is the King?"

"The same as the Emperor," replied the Baroness. "You see, Austria and Hungary have been united under one government, and the King of Hungary is Emperor of Austria. There were many wars fought before this arrangement was made, and all the different peoples of the empire agreed to live peaceably together."

"How long has Hungary had a king?" asked Marushka.

"Oh, for years and years," said the Baroness. "It was about the twelfth century when the Aranybulla was made, which gave to the nobles the right to rebel if the king did not live up to the constitution. See! There are the barracks and the soldiers drilling. The country boys who come up to be trained are sometimes so stupid that they don't know their right foot from the left. So the sergeant ties a wisp of hay on the right foot and a wisp of straw on the left. Instead of saying, right-left, to teach them to march, he says szelma-szalma. Isn't it droll?"

"What is that building by the river?" asked Marushka. "The one with the little turrets and the tower before which the geese are swinging?"

"That, my little goose girl, is the Agricultural Building, and should you go inside you would find specimens of every kind of food raised in Hungary. But here we are at the hotel where we shall spend the night. You must have some supper and then hurry to bed, for to-morrow is the fête day of St. Stephen, and all must be up early to see the procession."

Marushka was so sleepy the next day that she could only yawn and rub her eyes when the maid called her at five o'clock to dress for the fête.

The twentieth of August, the feast of St. Stephen, is the greatest fête of the year in Hungary.

Marushka and Banda Bela were very much excited over it, for they had often heard of the fête but had never supposed they would have the good fortune to see it.

"Come, children," the Baroness said as they hastily ate their breakfast. "We must hurry away. Hear the bells and the cannon! Every church in the city is ringing its chimes. We must be in the Palace Square by seven or we will miss some of the sights."

"I think the High-Born Baron and his Gracious Lady are the finest sights we shall see," whispered Banda Bela to Marushka, and the Baroness caught the words and smiled at him. There was a subtle sympathy between these two, the high and the lowly, the Magyar noblewoman and the Gypsy boy, a sympathy born, perhaps, of the love of music which swayed them both.

Marushka felt wonderfully fine as their carriage rolled into the Palace Square, where the procession in honour of St. Stephen was forming. It was a gorgeous sight, for all were dressed in their gayest attire, and officers, soldiers, prelates, and guard of honour from the palace made a continual line of conflicting hues.

While the procession was passing Marushka almost held her breath, then, as the golden radiance of colour flashing in the sunlight streamed past, she clapped her hands in glee, and cried:

"Oh, your Gracious High-Bornness! Isn't it splendid! How glad I am that St. Stephen is the Magyar saint and that I am a Magyar!" The child's eyes were shining, her cheeks flushed, her hair a golden coronet in the sunshine, and she looked like a beautiful little princess.

At the sound of her voice an officer in uniform, who was passing, turned and looked into the child's face, then glanced from her to the Baroness, who waved her hand in greeting. He doffed his cap and then came to the carriage.

"Good morning, Count. It is long since I have seen you in Buda-Pest. Are you not marching to-day?" the Baroness said.

"No, Madame." The officer had a kind face, but it seemed very sad to Marushka. She thought she had seen him before, but did not remember where until Banda Bela whispered that it was the officer who had given them money for Marushka's top boots at the fair.

"I was on duty at the palace this morning, but am returning home at once. My wife is not very well," he said.

"It is long since I have seen her. Will she receive me if I drive out to your home?" the Baroness asked.

"She will be glad to see you," he said, "though she sees but few since her ill health."

"I shall drive out to-day with these little folk, to whom I am showing the sights," said the Baroness.

The count's eyes fell upon Banda Bela, and he gave a quick smile.

"Why, this is the little genius who played the violin so wonderfully well down at the village fair," he said; and Banda Bela smiled, well pleased at being remembered.

"The little girl is yours?" he asked. The Baroness hesitated.

"No," she said. "She is not mine. She is the child of a friend of mine." Marushka wondered what good Aszszony Semeyer would say to hear herself spoken of as a friend of the Baroness, and, amused, she looked up at the Count with a beaming smile. He started a little and then stared at her fixedly, just as the Baroness with a hasty adieu bade the coachman drive on.

"Madame," he asked quickly, as the horses started. "Who is the friend whose child this is?" The Baroness looked back at him over her shoulder.

"That I cannot tell you now," she said. "This afternoon at your castle I will ask you to tell me!"

34

CHAPTER IX

"OH, THE EYES OF MY MOTHER!"

"OH, High-Born Graciousness, what is that beautiful street we are driving into?" asked Marushka, as they drove out in the afternoon, and the coachman turned the horses into a magnificent avenue.

"This is Andrássy-ut, the famous boulevard, which leads to the park," replied the Baroness. "We are driving toward Os Budavará, the Park of Buda-Pest, and it is one of the most beautiful sights in the world."

As she spoke they entered the park, and the children gazed in wonder at its beauty. Swans floated on the miniature lakes; in the feathery green woods bloomed exquisite Persian lilacs, children played on the green grass beneath the willows or ran to and fro over the rustic bridges. On the Corso the fashionables drove up and down in the smartest of costumes, their turnouts as well appointed as any in Paris or London. The men were many of them in uniform, the women, some of them with slanting dark eyes almost like Japanese, were graceful and elegant.

"The skating fêtes held in the park in winter are the most beautiful things you can imagine," said the Baroness. "The whole country is white with snow. Frost is in the air, the blood tingles with the cold. Ice kiosks are erected everywhere, and coloured lights are hung up until the whole place seems like fairyland, and the skaters, dressed from top to toe in furs, look like fairy people skimming over the ice."

"It must be beautiful," said Marushka.

"But what is that man playing?"

"The taragato, the old-fashioned Magyar clarinet," was the answer, and the old instrument seemed to tell tales of warlike days, its deep tones rolling out like the wind of the forest. A boy near by played an impudent little tilinka (flageolet), and Banda Bela said:

"That never sounded like real music to me; only the violin sings. It is like the wind in the trees, the rustle of the grass on the moor, the dash of the waves on the shore, the voice of the mother to her child."

"Banda Bela, you are poet as well as musician," said the Baroness. "You shall never go back to Harom Szölöhoz to live. You shall stay with me. I will sing to your music, and you shall study music till you are the greatest violin player in all Hungary."

"When a Gypsy child comes into the world they say his mother lays him on the ground and at one side places a purse and at the other a violin," said Banda Bela. "To one side or other the baby will turn his head. If he turns to the purse he will be a thief, if he turns to the violin he will earn his living by music. My mother said she would give me no chance to choose ill, but an old woman near by laid forth both the purse and the violin and I turned my head to the violin and reached for it with my baby hand. When they placed the bow in my hand I grasped it so tight they could scarce take it from me."

"Banda Bela," said Marushka, and her tone was pettish. "You like your violin better than you do me!" The boy laughed.

"My violin has earned you many a supper, Little One; do not dislike it!"

"Oh, Your Graciousness, what are those strange things?" cried Marushka. "They are not automobiles, are they?"

"No, my child, they are the new steam thrashing machines which the government has just bought, and is teaching the peasants to use instead of the old-fashioned ways of thrashing. Now we are getting into the country. See how beautifully the road winds along the Danube! Is it not a wonderful river? There is a famous waltz called the 'Beautiful Blue Danube' and the river is certainly as blue as the sky. See that queer little cemetery among the hills. I have often wondered why some of the gravestones in the village cemeteries had three feathers and coloured ribbons on them."

"If you please, Your Graciousness," said Banda Bela, "I can tell you. That is for the grave of a girl who has died after she was of an age to be married, yet for whom no one had offered the buying money. Aszszony Semeyer told me that."

"Aszszony Semeyer told me that every peasant kept a wooden shovel hung upon the wall of his house with which to throw in the last shovelful of earth upon his loved ones," said Marushka with a shudder. "Ugh! I didn't like that."

"Very few people like to think about death," said the Baroness. "See that thicket of prickly pears beside the road? Once when I was a little girl and very, very naughty, I ran away from my nurse and to hide from her I jumped over the wall and landed in just such a thicket as that. I think the pears must be naughty, too, for they liked that little girl and would not let her go. The thorns pricked her legs and tore her frock and scratched her hands when she tried to get her skirts loose, until she cried with pain and called 'Kerem jojoro ide' to her nurse."

"I did not think the Gracious Baroness was ever naughty," said Marushka.

"The Gracious Baroness was quite like other little girls, my dear," she said, smiling. "Ah, I have a little twinge of toothache!" she exclaimed.

"That is too bad." Marushka was all sympathy. "Aszszony Semeyer says that if you will always cut your finger nails on Friday you will never have toothache."

"Is that so? Then I shall certainly try it," said the Baroness soberly. "Do you see the gleam of white houses between the trees? Those are the beautiful villas and castles of the Svabhegy, the hill overlooking the Danube, and here live many of my very good friends.

"I am going to visit one of them for a little while and you must be good, quiet children and sit in the carriage while I go in to make my call. Then, perhaps, I will take you in for a few moments to see the house, for it is a very beautiful one. See! here we are at the gate," as the carriage turned into a beautifully ornamented gateway, above which was carved the legend: If you love God and your Country, enter; with malice in your heart, go your way.

The driveway wound through beautiful grounds, and through the trees were seen glimpses of the Danube. The house itself was white and stood at the crest of the hill overlooking the river.

"This place belongs to the Count Ándrassy," said the Baroness. "He has also another place in the Aföld and is very wealthy. When my grandfather went to visit his grandfather in the old days, they once took the wheels from his carriage and tied them to the tops of the tallest poplar trees on the estate to prevent his leaving. Another time they greased the shafts with wolf fat, so that the horses would not allow themselves to be harnessed up, for they are so afraid of the wolf smell. Still another time they hid his trunks in the attic so that it was three months before my grandfather finally got away.

"That was old-fashioned hospitality. Here we are at the door. Sit quietly here and I will return," and the Baroness sprang down. There was a swish of her silken skirts and the front door closed behind her.

The children chattered gaily to each other of all they had seen and heard since they had left Harom Szölöhoz, and Marushka said:

"It seems so long since we have left the village, Banda Bela; somehow it seems as if we would never go back."

"I think you never will." Banda Bela spoke a little sadly. "Were you happy there, Little One?"

"Oh, yes," she said brightly. "I was happy with you and Aszszony Semeyer. Only, when I saw other children with their mothers, there was the ache right here—" she laid her hand on her heart.

"I know," said Banda Bela. "I have that always. Only when I play my violin do I forget."

"But I cannot play the violin, nor can I do anything, only embroider that horrible Himmelbelt," and Marushka pouted, while Banda Bela laughed at her.

"Think how proud you will be some day to show that Himmelbelt to your husband," he said, but just then the Baroness and the Count came out of the house together.

"What do you think?" the Baroness asked the Count.

"I think you are right, but Maria shall decide," he answered. "We will say nothing to her and her heart will speak."

"Come in, children," said the Baroness, who looked strangely excited. Her eyes shone and her cheeks were flushed, while the Count's face was pale as death and he looked strangely at Marushka.

"Banda Bela," said the Baroness, "the Countess is not very well. She loves music as you and I do, and I want you to come in and play for her. She is very sad. Once she lost her dear little daughter, and you may play some gentle little songs for her. It may give her pleasure. It is a beautiful thing, Banda Bela, to give pleasure to those who are sad."

The Baroness chattered on as they entered the house. Marushka looked up at the Count's face. Sad as it was she felt drawn toward him. She saw him watching her closely and smiled up at him with the pretty, frank smile which always lighted up her face so charmingly.

"High-Born Count," she said shyly, "I have to thank you for the first present I ever received in all my life."

"What was that, Little One?" he asked.

"The top boots which Banda Bela bought for me at the fair at Harom Szölöhoz. They were bought with the florin you gave to Banda Bela for his playing. They were so nice!" She dimpled prettily.

"I am glad they gave you pleasure. Come, we will go in and hear Banda Bela play," said the Count, holding out his hand. Marushka slipped her hand into his and he led her into the house, entering by the large hall, on the walls of which hung deer horns and wolf heads, while a huge stuffed wolf stood at one end, holding a lamp in his paws. The Count was a great sportsman and had shot many of these animals himself in the forests of the Transylvania.

Banda Bela tuned his violin and then began to play. It seemed to Marushka as if she had never before heard him play so beautifully. Many things he played, all soft and dreamy, with a gentle, haunting sadness through them, until at last he struck into a peculiar melody, a sort of double harmony of joy and sorrow, which he had never played before.

"What is that, Banda Bela?" demanded the Baroness. "Who wrote it, what are the words?"

"If you please, Your Graciousness"—the boy flushed, "it is but a Gypsy song of sorrow. The words are but in my own heart."

"Strange boy," she thought, but at that moment the door opened and a lady hastily entered the room. She was tall and very beautiful, with great masses of corn-coloured hair and deep blue eyes, but her face had a look of terrible sadness.

"Arpád!" she exclaimed. "What is this music? It makes me weep for my lost one and I am nearly blind with weeping now." Her eyes, seeking her husband's, fell upon Marushka, who during the music had been leaning against the Count, his arm around her. The Countess' eyes travelled up and down the little figure, then sought her husband's face with a sort of eager, frightened questioning.

"Arpád!" she cried. "Arpád! Who is this child?"

"Maria, my dearest! I have brought her here that you may tell me who she is," he said, trying to speak calmly.

She drew the little girl toward her and Marushka went willingly and stood looking into the sweet face of the Countess.

"Such a likeness," whispered the Baroness. "They are as like as two sisters."

Then, all in a moment, the Countess gathered Marushka into her arms and covered the child's face with kisses. "You are mine," she cried, tears streaming down her face. "Mine! Arpád! I know it is our little daughter come back to us after all these years. My heart tells me it is she!"

Marushka looked frightened for a moment, then she clung around her mother's neck, and the Baroness quietly drew Banda Bela from the room. From the hall the sound of the Gypsy boy's violin came as he played, with all his soul in his touch, the song of his father:

"The hills are so blue,

The sun so warm,

The wind of the moor so soft and so kind!

Oh, the eyes of my mother,

The warmth of her breast,

The breath of her kiss on my cheek, alas!"

THE END